Other Books by Tony Seton

The Larger Reality / The Realm of Higher Consciousness
Do You Mind?
The Ultimate App
Covid Blue
True Tens / Seven Women of Beautiful Character
The Flight of KAL 007
The Bright Wise Solution
Mokki's Peak
Silent Alarm
Deki-san
Equinox
No Soap, Radio
Paradise Pond
Selected Writings
Jennifer
The Francie LeVillard Mysteries - Volumes I - X
The Francie LeVillard Mysteries - The Early Years
Trinidad Head
Just Imagine
The Autobiography of John Dough, Gigolo
Silver Lining
Mayhem
The Omega Crystal/New Moves
Truth Be Told
Musings on Sherlock Holmes
Say It Write
Is There a Why?
13 Days of Fear
The Brink
Dead as a Doorbell
The Quality Interview / Getting It Right on Both Sides of the Mic
From Terror to Triumph / The Herma Smith Curtis Story
Don't Mess with the Press / How to Write, Produce, and Report Quality Television News
Right Car, Right Price

Thought So

Thought So

A screenplay by Tony Seton

Based in part on a true story

Carmel, California

September 2024

This is an original screenplay based in part on the author's true life experiences. The characters in this book are fictional, except those expressly cited via historical reference.

Thought So

ISBN-13: 978-1-7375932-0-1

Printed in the United States of America

Author's Note

When I was ten years old, I was throwing a baseball back and forth with a friend who was maybe twenty feet away. At one point, after I had thrown the ball to him, I was looking down adjusting my glove and did not see him throw the ball back. Suddenly, without being cognizant of the ball in the air, I raised my glove in a flash and caught it three inches before it would have struck my left eye with considerable force.

I knew at the time that it was something large. I also knew that it was outside of my then-understanding of how life worked. At that age and my upbringing, I knew nothing to explain how I had saved myself from what would have been a serious injury. But it had happened.

Six decades later, after countless experiences of what I used to call coincidence and later serendipity and synchronicity, I understand that there is a *larger reality* that is operating. That's what I call it for lack of a better term.

A few years ago, while working on a book for a client, I chose to refer to it as The Force.

Everyone would know that reference. That afternoon, when I was out walking the dawg, a van drove by me, and across its back window was a large-letter decal that read **May The Force Be With You**.

There have been many moments like that, indications that I have taken to mean that I was on my right path. I believe that a larger reality is operating for everything and everyone, and that those who recognize and trust in it have a more functional, more satisfying – sometimes exhilarating – life.

I bring this up because it's all about energy. Our body is made of atoms which are energy. Our body runs on energy. Breathing, heart beating, balance, motion, vision, hearing, taste, touch, smell are all energy. As are all of our thoughts and our feelings.

We also have the capacity to sense and parse the energy of other people and of situations. Those people who take responsibility for their own lives have enhanced awareness of the world around them.

The essence of this story is that vaccinated people of higher consciousness can read the thoughts of other people. I know this for a fact.

Tony Seton
Carmel, California

The Players

Brett Whitson - Broadcast Journalist

Nurse

Leslie - Psychiatrist

Earl - Accountant

"James Mason"

Gladys - Leslie's partner

Missy Blaine - Consultant

Franklin - Data whiz

Private Dick

Eddie Silkwood - Police lieutenant

Missy's Client

Spiff Jerkins - TV station exec

Hobart Lipscomb - TV station exec

"George Burns"

Volunteers - Students - Waitpersons

Thought So

SCENE ONE

It's late morning on a spring day. Throughout the scene, soft classical music is playing from the car audio system, and credits are showing when there is no action. Brett Whitson is in his car in a line waiting to get his second Covid vaccination. As the line moves forward, he first encounters a volunteer who hands him a form on a clip board to fill out.

FIRST VOLUNTEER

Thank you for getting vaccinated.

Shortly thereafter a second volunteer comes to him, takes the form on the billboard, confirming that it has been filled out and signed.

SECOND VOLUNTEER

We really appreciate you getting vaccinated.

The line moves forward and Brett stops next to a tent. A third volunteer comes out and hands him an ID card that has his information on it, confirming his two vaccinations.

THIRD VOLUNTEER

(Looking down to confirm the name) Thank you, Mr. Whitson, for coming in for being vaccinated. Have a healthy life.

Brett is directed by arrows and more volunteers to drive through to where the vaccinations are given. There is no waiting. He pulls up next to a tent, and a nurse comes out.

NURSE

(Smiling) Good morning, Mr. Whitson. Now this being your second vaccination, I think you know that it doesn't hurt.

BRETT

Piece 'o cake. (Gets the shot; smiling, no grimace) You folks seem to be in such a great mood.

NURSE

Yes. It's so much better than working in a hospital.

BRETT

That's why everyone is so gracious and cheery?

NURSE

(Sighs) Well think about it. Here we are helping people who have the intelligence and sense of community to protect themselves. They won't get Covid; they won't wind up in a hospital ER. It even saves them from possible dying.

BRETT

I trust the people who come through are grateful.

NURSE

(She smiles, stretches her arms out to the scene around her) We all are.

BRETT

Thank you. Thank you for the shots and the spirit.

NURSE

You're so welcome. Now you drive over there and wait for fifteen minutes to make sure you don't have any reaction to the shot.

BRETT

I didn't have any the first time. I feel fine. Do many people have negative effects?

NURSE

Very few. The two I heard about, it was just a case of nerves. Like they were overanxious about a possible reaction. Some deep breaths, a cup of water, and they were done.

BRETT

Dunno what people get afraid of.

NURSE

Oh, you would be surprised at some people. The misinformation they've heard.

BRETT

From their friends?

NURSE

Yes, and social media. It's a wonder anyone is vaccinated with all the lies out there.

BRETT

I guess it's testimony about those people who didn't feel well still had the courage to get their shots anyway. That's a good sign.

NURSE

Yes, you're right. (She looks hard at Brett) Um, you look familiar.

BRETT

(Smiles) I used to be on the news.

NURSE

That's right. But you're not anymore? What happened, if I might ask?

BRETT

It's all right. I disagreed with the management. In fact, over what we were talking about. They wanted me to report on fake remedies - you know, what Trump was pushing - and I refused. They said I could say they weren't proven but people should know about them. But as you know, the stuff he was pushing was a lot worse, far more dangerous than simply unproven. So I was fired.

NURSE

(Looking at him with new respect) I'm sorry, but good for you. People could get seriously ill. Like taking bleach. That's crazy.

BRETT

That was my feeling. I wasn't going to help people kill themselves, by using the wrong stuff, and, even if they didn't get sick, thinking that they didn't need to get properly vaccinated.

NURSE

Do you mind if I ask, what you're going to do now?

BRETT

No, I don't mind. I don't know what I'm going to do. I've been making notes on a possible book about what's happened to the news. It's not what it used to be. It's about ratings and sales...money instead of serving the community.

NURSE

Well good luck to you...and stay healthy.

BRETT

Thank you, and you keep saving lives.

SCENE TWO

It's that afternoon. Brett is sitting on the deck outside his cabin in the Carmel Highlands. Through some trees, he looks out a half-mile to the Pacific Ocean while on his cellphone.

BRETT

Leslie, you're a psychiatrist, which means you went to medical school. Are you telling me you haven't gotten vaccinated yet?

Leslie is at her desk in a very nice office. She's working on her lunch break and conversing on a speaker phone.

LESLIE

Hey, there are a lot of people who actually work on people physically in hospitals and clinics, not to mention first responders, who haven't gotten shots.

BRETT

Yes, and that's nuts. You saw the story about the

153 staffers at Houston Methodist Hospital. They sued the hospital for requiring that they get vaccinated.

LESLIE

I missed that. What happened?

BRETT

Their suit said the vaccines were experimental and dangerous. A judge said that was false and irrelevant noting that the federal government gave companies the right to require their employees be vaccinated.

LESLIE

Ouch.

BRETT

In their suit, they equated the mandate to medical experimentation during the Holocaust. The judge, rightly, called that "reprehensible".

LESLIE

(Shaking her head) I can't argue with the judge on that one.

BRETT

So Les, why aren't you getting the shots? They seem to be hugely effective with virtually no side effects.

LESLIE

It's the virtually that worries me.

BRETT

What about your partner? Has she gotten vaccinated?

LESLIE

(Takes a deep breath and lets it out noisily.)

BRETT

Oh, she's why you won't get poked.

LESLIE

To tell you the truth, I probably would get them if Glad weren't so fired up about it.

BRETT

What's her concern? You're young and healthy.

LESLIE

(Resisting) She says I might be risking our child.

BRETT

You don't have any children.

LESLIE

But if I wanted to have a child, she might not be

healthy. Might suffer from autism.

BRETT

(Brett takes an audible deep breath) You know better than that, Leslie.

LESLIE

Yeah, I do. But I'm not ready to break up our relationship over it.

BRETT

I understand. So let me ask you, have you read anything about side effects from the vaccinations?

LESLIE

Is this a test?

BRETT

No, dear girl, it's 'cause I wanted to know if people experienced any weirdness from their shots.

LESLIE

You had the Pfizer shots, both of them?

BRETT

Yes. The second this morning.

LESLIE

Well, it seems those have the least. Some people have felt sick or had a sore shoulder, but very, very few had any serious issues. Why, Brett? You're feeling okay, aren't you?

BRETT

Yeah, I feel fine. (Silent for a moment.) Actually, better than fine.

LESLIE

What does that mean?

BRETT

I'm not sure how to describe it...

LESLIE

(Joking) You mean without sounding weird, weirder than usual?

BRETT

Thank you, yes. I won't say euphoric, but better than usual. My mind isn't going to things I might normally worry about.

LESLIE

Like what are you going to do with your life?

BRETT

As a matter of fact, over the last couple of hours, that issue seems to have evaporated for me.

LESLIE

(Serious) Wow. That's a big deal, for anyone, but especially for you. I know how you were feeling.

BRETT

Yeah, it's purdy dang neat.

LESLIE

It not from grass or hash?

BRETT

Nope. Haven't touched the stuff.

LESLIE

And this is since you got the second shot?

BRETT

Uh-huh.

LESLIE

How long after that you started feeling some effects, that you realized that you were feeling so good, not worried?

BRETT

My goodness, you did go to medical school. Majored in diagnostics, didn't you?

LESLIE

I'm asking the questions, my friend.

BRETT

Yes you are. Thank you, Leslie.

LESLIE

And?

BRETT

I waited the 15 minutes for aftereffects, and all I noticed as I was driving home the forty-five minutes from the site was that I wasn't feeling rushed.

LESLIE

Didn't drive as fast as usual?

BRETT

I drove the speed limit. And I, I felt less competitive with the other drivers.

LESLIE

You were always a safe driver, Brett, but like most males, you'd rather pass than be passed.

(Waits) But that was different today?

BRETT

It was.

LESLIE

What else?

BRETT

I felt, I don't know, lighter.

LESLIE

Dizzy?

BRETT

No, not at all. In fact, my vision seemed clearer, and I wasn't as focused.

LESLIE

Looked less, saw more.

BRETT

Yeah, like that.

LESLIE

Okay, and when you got home, did you notice anything different?

BRETT

I felt more present. More grounded, but not

heavier. It was easier to walk. I moved very easily and not in a hurry. Does that tell you anything?

LESLIE

You mean, are you dead and just haven't fallen over?

BRETT

If that was it, I would recommend it broadly.

LESLIE

(Laughs) Okay, I haven't read or seen or heard anything like what you're describing. On the other hand, I certainly can't deride it.

BRETT

Yeah, I wasn't worried either.

LESLIE

Brett, my dear friend, I have a client who always gets here early and I can only make him wait so long. Let's get together, or at least talk this evening. And please, don't hesitate to call my if this feels uncomfortable, or scary, in any way. You have my special number. Call me. If there is an issue, I could explain it to another professional if need be.

BRETT

Dinner soon?

LESLIE

Promise. Love you. Bye.

BRETT

Love you, too.

SCENE THREE

Later that afternoon, Brett is working at his desk. Looking over his shoulder at different Internet sites and the notes he is making on a pad on his desk, it's clear he's looking up side effects reports. The phone rings. He looks at the display, smiles, and answers it. It's his friend Earl calling from his car.

BRETT

Hey bro, how's tricks?

EARL

Hah! I'll bet you dinner you don't know the origin of that expression.

BRETT

It would have to be In-and-Out Burger. Remember, I'm unemployed.

EARL

Pshaw. I'm your accountant and I know how much you have socked away. And I have no doubt you'll get at least a half-a-mil from those dumb schmucks who will have to pay for the unlawful breach of contract in canning you.

BRETT

Well, all right.

EARL

All right you give up, right?

BRETT

I mean I'll take you to In-and-Out.

EARL

Double hah of your choice of In-and-Out when I tell you the origin of the phrase.

BRETT

Now I really haven't a clue.

EARL

Good. "How's tricks" comes from asking a lady of the evening if she's turning a lot of tricks.

BRETT

You're kidding. I know you're an accountant and could never have made that up. And I love it relative to the In-and-Out reference. You must wonder if I knew the answer when I chose the restaurant.

EARL

It's not a restaurant. It's fast food joint. Okay, so I'm driving back from Saratoga, and just getting on 156. I'll be in Monterey or Carmel, your choice, in twenty minutes. Where shall it be?

BRETT

Mission Ranch. I'll call for a res on the deck.

EARL

Good choice. See you in a few.

SCENE FOUR

Brett and Earl are sitting at an outside table on the deck at Mission Ranch.

EARL

I gotta tell ya, that drive on 101 is downright scary. I was doing eighty in the middle lane - speed limit is sixty-five - and cars are flying by me on both sides. They were all but on top of each other. Remember when we were kids, it was a car length apart for every ten miles an hour? I had people on my tail who were maybe a car-length away. I moved over to the right-hand lane for the rest of the trip. That was why the trip was ten minutes later than it should have been.

BRETT

I know. I used to enjoy driving. Would drive out to Yosemite in the morning, took four hours, have lunch at the Ahwahnee, walk around the valley for a few hours, and then drive back.

Today I feel like going to Big Sur or other travel destinations only when they're out of season. What do you think is going on?

EARL

(Shakes his head slowly for several seconds) I don't know, but it's funny – not ha-ha funny – that you should ask because I've been thinking about this the last couple of months. I think I noticed something longer ago, but I'm seeing it more and more in different venues and situations. (Leans forward resting his forearms on the table) I don't know what it is, but it's feeling like things are out of synch, like we're coming off the rails.

BRETT

Who's "we"?

EARL

Not us, you and me, but society, and maybe the world.

BRETT

What have you noticed?

EARL

Some of it is heavy, like the dangerous driving. Did you know that during the pandemic, the number of miles driven was way down, but the number of roadway fatalities was way up? The number of mass shootings is up and climbing, everywhere in the country; which sort of explains how gun sales are going through the roof. And to first-time owners.

BRETT

Have you seen any change in your business? The people you work with? Your clients?

EARL

That's another thing. Most of our people who were working from home have said they were reluctant to come into the office. Even three or two days a week. And it's hard to argue with them because they were more efficient during the last year.

BRETT

What else? Were your clients asking for anything different?

EARL

(Grimaces) Yes. Many of them, especially those who don't need to play games, are pushing us to file riskier returns. They have plenty of money, ridiculously so, and they're all but asking to be audited.

BRETT

What are you doing about it?

EARL

At our weekly executives meeting, I insisted that we get letters from the clients agreeing that they have been fully and accurately apprised of possible issues that auditors might raise and that they will take responsibility for any reversals and penalties.

BRETT

How are the clients reacting?

EARL

In a word...scared. It's like they think their survival depends on making and keeping more money and they have to file returns that they see as very risky.

BRETT

That doesn't make a lot of sense, does it?

EARL

That's my point. It doesn't make sense. And there's a lot of that going around.

BRETT

Yessir. When you look at what's been going on

in politics, which most people don't have the stomach for, understandably, many intelligent people are seriously worried about the future of our democracy. And with good reason. So many people are voting against their own best interests. And look at the people in Congress who are clearly acting to preserve their seats but at the expense of the national well-being. Also, we see how extreme the far right is going, but what about the far left, they want strip the names Washington, Jefferson, Lincoln, and Roosevelt from public buildings.

EARL

And defund the police, for goodness' sake.

BRETT

Plus parents are supporting their seven-year-olds who say they want to change genders. I don't think I even knew what gender meant at that age.

EARL

I know. The far left is almost more frightening than there being maybe ten million AR15-style weapons in the United States.

BRETT

(Ponders) What is happening? Where do you

think we are headed?

EARL

That's the thing. I don't know. It's very bizarre. As I said, it doesn't make any sense. What happens when what we are doing doesn't make sense?

BRETT

Do you think it's connected with Covid?

EARL

Good question. But I think we need another bottle of that De Tierra Pinot.

BRETT

That is good, isn't it?

Brett gets the attention of the waiter and points to the bottle.

EARL

I think whatever it is started a while back, but it has been picking up speed. I would imagine that the pandemic played a part in it, maybe pushing people back on themselves, forcing them to think about their lives, what they were doing, and wondering if they wanted to go back to what they were doing or to figure out something else.

BRETT

I think you're right. But I don't have any idea what the whole picture looks like. Do you?

Earl shakes his head slowly again.

SCENE FIVE

Brett is in the bathroom, getting ready for bed. After brushing his teeth and staring at them in the mirror, he looks in the mirror at his upper left arm. Then he looks down at his arm and touches it gently. He smiles. Obviously no pain. He takes a deep breath and lets it out. He goes to leave the bathroom and flicks off the light. Putting the screen in darkness.

SCENE SIX

Brett is in bed, asleep. The camera tightens in on his face and forehead. Then the shot dissolves into a dream.

SCENE SEVEN

Brett, wearing his pajama pants as before, in a structure-less realm. He has no feeling of hot or cold, or any emotions. He sees people moving around at a distance. Then he realizes that walking next to him is a James Mason-looking character, who is wearing an expensive business suit. And while we can hear what they are saying, their lips aren't moving. They are reading each other's thoughts and it is very natural.

BRETT

My first thought is being on a set out of *Heaven Can Wait,* puffy clouds, no sound. And you looking like Buck Henry's boss in the movie. Am I dead? I don't feel any different.

MASON

No, you're not dead, Brett. You're here to learn what is happening and your role in it.

BRETT

That sounds rather daunting.

MASON

It is. You are on the beginning of a trip - a new life in a way - and you need to understand it.

BRETT

Okay. Ready.

MASON

Before you went to sleep, you were wondering about possible side effects of the Covid vaccinations.

BRETT

Wondering? Yes. I'm wondering if you were listening in on my conversations?

MASON

With Leslie and then Earl. Not listening in, really?

BRETT

What really?

MASON

We listened in on your thoughts.

BRETT

Hmm. So this is an after effect of the vaccination. My thoughts are readable, and for some reason you, whoever you are, have decided to listen in mine.

MASON

Yes, and don't you find it interesting that this doesn't upset you?

BRETT

Well, dreams aren't real life, are they?

MASON

Actually they are, but this isn't really a dream. You are sleeping, but your mind is awake and you are thinking and we are having this conversation.

BRETT

Is this happening to a lot of people? That people who have been vaccinated - my guess is had both shots - are discovering that they can hear other people's thoughts?

MASON

That's right.

BRETT

Who are those people?

MASON

Ah yes, it's not just they have been vaccinated,

both shots. We have assessed people based on a CQ scale.

BRETT

CQ?

MASON

Oh, sorry, yes. That stands consciousness quotient. Instead of measuring intelligence, according to the IQ scale, we wanted to identify those people who were not only bright but also thoughtful, moral, compassionate...and of course truthful.

BRETT

(Smiles humbly) Why thank you, I think.

MASON

Oh most certainly. And not only do you have those qualities - which you demonstrated so visibly in dealing with the management at the television station who wanted you to lie to your viewers to try to sway them away from the facts - but you were very good at your job and that should come in very handy as the show goes on.

BRETT

What is the show?

MASON

Do you remember Ed Sullivan?

BRETT

Somewhat.

MASON

He was known for saying he had 'a really big shoow'. That's what we've got.

BRETT

What is the purpose of this really big show?

MASON

To get the people back on track.

BRETT

What does that mean?

MASON

That's not for me to tell you. I was just sent to meet you to tell you of your new path. Well, to tell you that you're on it and that everything is all right. But you seem to know that already. And good for you.

BRETT

Will I remember this dream, cognitively, or will it just be part of me?

MASON

You will remember it, but not as a dream. It is what you really experienced.

BRETT

How will I be able to communicate with you?

MASON

You won't but you will not need to. You won't see me again. I've done my part.

BRETT

Will there be others?

MASON

When it's time. When you need more input.

BRETT

Will it be in a dream again? Or how will I know them?

MASON

You will know.

SCENE EIGHT

Brett is lying in bed, awake, looking thoughtful and at peace. The clock by his bed clicks over from 6:59 to 7:00. A few seconds later, his phone rings. It's a model of an old landline, without a display.

BRETT

Good morning, Leslie.

LESLIE

Hey, I called you on your antique thing. How did you know it was me?

BRETT

Thank you for calling, dear Leslie. And yes, I feel fine. Quite fine, in fact.

LESLIE

Hrumph. Well, I guess that's a good thing anyway. None of the side effects thing you were worried about, right?

BRETT

Nothing to worry about, no. Thank you.

LESLIE

(Carefully) You sound different, Brett. Are you sure you're all right?

BRETT

Couldn't be better. How are you this lovely morning?

LESLIE

"Lovely"? It's, um, foggy and cold. Grrr, are you taking Ecstasy again?

BRETT

(Laughs) No, Leslie. Lovely because the fog does such wonderful things for the flora. My yard lady refers to it as pseudo rain. (Changes his tone) Hey, didn't you say that you and Gladys were going up to Tassajara tomorrow?

LESLIE

(Unenthusiastic) That's the plan. (Sighs) I suppose we will.

BRETT

Just up for the day?

LESLIE

(Curious) Yes. Why?

BRETT

I thought you might like to leave Bogie with me. I'll take him for a run on the beach. What's up with you, Les? Bogie and I are great buds. I won't be jobless forever. You might as well take advantage of his favorite sitter while you can.

LESLIE

(Mostly satisfied) Yeah, sure. He'd like that.

BRETT

And I really am fine. I got eight hours of sleep last night. I rarely get more than six. And I woke up in a good mood.

LESLIE

Hah. That's because you haven't read the news.

BRETT

Maybe. What's in the news?

LESLIE

Haven't a clue. It's too depressing first thing in the morning. I don't know how you do it... (Suspicion returns) when you do it...which is usually every day.

BRETT

Yes I do. I'm a real journalist. I keep an emotional distance from the muck and the mire.

LESLIE

What else is there?

BRETT

There's that. (Pauses) Probably reports about how the antivaxxers have persuaded ever more Trumpists and QAnoners not to save their lives.

LESLIE

Is that good news?

BRETT

Some would say they deserve to get Covid and have to be hospitalized and maybe die.

LESLIE

Are you "some"?

BRETT

Leslie, you're sounding like a shrink. And I don't want to condemn someone in my thoughts to suffer that way. Especially people I care about, like you, who is letting someone else make the decision for you not to get vaccinated, especially as you know you should.

LESLIE

There's something different about you this morning, Brett.

BRETT

Probably the vaccine.

LESLIE

Are you feeling any after-effects from the shots this morning?

BRETT

Maybe. I was really on a high from that experience. I think maybe the four people I encountered in the process, with the forms and getting poked, all thanked me, genuinely, for being vaccinated.

LESLIE

(Hearing him.) Really? I can hear that it was important to you.

BRETT

It was meaningful. These people are volunteers. They know how important it is to reach the herd immunity level, so everyone who comes through, everyone they process, is moving us closer to that. Leslie, I would never tell you what you must do, you know that, but if you got sick because you listened to Glad instead of doing what you know you should...I would be very disappointed in you, and never speak another word to her.

LESLIE

You know what's different about you this morning? You're not angry or loud, in your tone or your words. You are in such a peaceful place. I've never known you not to show your emotions before, when something was important to you, and I know how important it is to you. I hear it in your words, but it's not with anger.

BRETT

Are you able to hear me better, what I'm saying?

LESLIE

Funny, or maybe it's not. I might have said that the anger I would have expected to hear would have underscored the importance you felt. But yes, I am able to take in what you are saying better. Maybe because I could simply hear you and not have to filter out the anger. I think I have to have another talk with her about this.

BRETT

Good girl, Leslie. What time are you going to bring Bogie to me tomorrow?

SCENE NINE

It's early afternoon and Brett is walking along the service road above the beach and below the houses of Carmel Meadows. He sees a very healthy woman jogging up the path in his direction. As she gets closer, he can see that she is also quite pretty. But then thirty feet away he sees that she is sporting a MAGA hat. He feels disappointment. When she reaches him, she gives him a big smile, pivots, and starts walking next to him.

ARIEL

Hi, Brett, I'm Ariel. I wear the hat because I'm undercover. The right-wingers look at me the same way you did, except more lasciviously and with no subtlety. But that gives me a chance to know what's going on with these yo-yos. I report to...well, you don't need to know that. (She puts her hand on his shoulder and gives him a little squeeze.) I think you need some more guidance about your new abilities.

BRETT

(Thought he should feel surprised, but he didn't) Yes, thank you, Ariel, a few things. Do I tell you or do you already know?

ARIEL

Yes and yes. You're vocalizing your thoughts will help you feel more familiar with some of the nuance.

BRETT

That makes sense. But if I might ask, are you dead?

ARIEL

(Laughs) If I was, I would have to be the best looking corpse you've ever seen. No, I'm alive. I'm with you. I got my jabs earlier so I have more experience.

BRETT

How nice. Okay, I don't want to waste your time. Two things. One is that I'm going to be with a good friend's dog tomorrow.

ARIEL

Bogie, Leslie's woof.

BRETT

Yes. And I was thinking that I could maybe share thoughts with him.

ARIEL

But of course. It's all about energy. That's what thoughts are. And you want to know if you can understand dog thoughts. (Brett nods.) Yes, of course. One of your acquisitions is a real-time language converter. It does more foreign languages, drunks who slur their words, and most animals.

BRETT

"Most"? Oh, only the animals with whom - or that - humans would have contact with. None of the creatures at 35,000 feet in the Mariana Trench.

ARIEL

Exactly.

BRETT

And the other question that came up today was when I went to the supermarket....

ARIEL

And when you were standing in line, you heard all those people recognizing - or thinking they recognized – you and saying all sorts of things that weren't even close to reality.

BRETT

Yes. I mean, I know that's the nature of the beast, being a public figure.

ARIEL

And being on television, (looks at him with raised eyebrows) and not so bad looking. And yes, I'm single but I never mix business with pleasure.

BRETT

Even though they were too far away from me to actually hear them say things to their friends, I was picking up their thoughts.

ARIEL

Nasty.

BRETT

One said, "I wonder why he's not on the news anymore." Another: "I saw on Facebook that he was having family issues." And "I heard it was drugs." Another: "My sister said he tried to go out with one of the high school cheerleaders."

ARIEL

I was a cheerleader; the cheerleader captain.

BRETT

Are you over seventeen? (Not a real question.)

ARIEL

And you want to know how you can keep the noise down, or out?

BRETT

It is a distraction. A lot of people thinking at the same time. It's just too much noise.

ARIEL

Very good.

BRETT

What "very good"?

ARIEL

You think smartly. You see the gaps in what you need to know.

BRETT

And?

ARIEL

And you simply have to focus-listen. Like tuning

in a radio station, you just tune into the person whose thoughts you want to hear, and the rest is filtered out. And you can turn them all off for a time. It's very easy. Like pushing the mute button. You'll see how it works when you have more exposure.

BRETT

So I can listen to what people are thinking by selecting the person or persons by deciding it in my mind.

ARIEL

Yes. You have complete control. You can have a lot of fun with it, too. Turn it on with a wink of your right eye, off with you left. You can set up any system of selections you want, change them anytime. It's all in your head, as the saying goes.

BRETT

Can anyone who wants to hear my thoughts?

ARIEL

No. Only if you want them to, and they have a level of consciousness high enough to be trusted to handle the ability.

BRETT

And have gotten the vaccinations.

ARIEL

But of course. No slowpokes. And only if you want them to. You need to be deliberately connected to have your thoughts heard by someone. If you don't want someone to listen in on you, all you have to do is decided you don't want to be heard and everyone will be blocked out. But when there is someone you want to be open to, you just have to think that. It doesn't necessarily mean that they will be listening, just that they are able to. And then it's not the pre-conceived thoughts or purposeful remarks. It is only what comes into your mind without deliberation. What's from your intuitive self. Your intuition is the voice of your soul.

BRETT

Ooh, I like that. It makes so much sense, and it feels so right. Thank you, Ariel. You're a dream.

Laughing, Ariel continues her run.

<u>*SCENE TEN*</u>

Mid-morning the next day. Brett walks out his front door and down the walk to greet Leslie getting out of her car. Bogie is looking out the back window at Brett, whining a happy hello.

BRETT

(Enthusiastic) Bogie...how good to see you, my friend.

Leslie opens the back door to let Bogie out. Bogie bounds out of the car to Brett who bends down and rubs Bogie's head as he licks Brett's face.

BRETT

We're gonna have a great day today, Bogie. Mano-a-mano. Go stir up some quiet numbers on the beach. Whaddaya say?

BOGIE

Woof, arf.

BRETT

(Stands up, takes the leash from Leslie) I don't think we'll need that. I always come when he calls me.

GLADYS

(From the front seat, scornfully) You and that dog!

BRETT

Hi, Glad. You and Les have a grand time up there with the yellow togas.

LESLIE

(Shoots him raised eyebrows as she gets back in the car) Oy. (In her seat, restarts the engine.) We should be back around 5:30.

BRETT

(Feigns surprise) Today? (Laughs) That's good. I have a class at seven tonight.

Leslie shakes her head, smiling, and drives away,

BRETT

(Waves at them and turns back to the house. To Bogie) You hungry?

BOGIE

(Talks without barking) Yum.

BRETT

(Smiles) This is gonna be fun.

BOGIE

Kibble.

BRETT

Better than kibble, my friend. I went to the Rio Grill last night and got some of their best bones and cooked them up for you.

BOGIE

Yum.

BRETT

But first I thought we'd head over to Carmel Beach. Shouldn't be a lot of people today, mid-week, and only the best of the breed - your breed - out on the sand.

BOGIE

Friends.

BRETT

That's right. Mostly the regulars, I expect.

BOGIE

Now.

BRETT

Yes, pal. I just have to get my coat and keys and lock the door. Do you need a drink of water before we go?

BOGIE

Go now.

BRETT

Yessir.

Just inside the door, Brett grabs his coat and keys, steps back out, closes and locks the door and they're on their way.

SCENE ELEVEN

Brett is walking down the beach. Not many people or dogs are out yet, but Bogie has found a couple of friends and they're having a good time. They're too far away from him for Brett to understand what they are saying. But as a couple whose dog is one of those romping in the surf with his friend, Brett begins to pick up their thoughts.

THE MAN

(Thinking) I don't know where this relationship is going. She's never happy with me.

THE WOMAN

(Thinking) He's not a bad man, but we just don't fit. I have a better relationship with the dog than with him. But Lucy is his dog. And she likes me better than her owner.

THE MAN

(Thinking) It pisses me off that Lucy is nicer to her than to me. What is it...a female thing?

THE WOMAN

(Aloud) I love it when there's no one on the beach like this.

THE MAN

Yeah, it's great. Lucy likes it, too.

THE WOMAN

She loves the other dogs on the beach.

THE MAN

And especially that golden lab.

THE WOMAN

That's Bogie.

THE MAN

Is that his owner?

THE WOMAN

No. His name is Brett, I think. He takes him down here a lot. But a couple of women own him.

THE MAN

So is he a dog-walker or something?

THE WOMAN

No. Well, maybe now. He used to be a news

anchorman on Channel Eight.

THE MAN

Oh, yes. I thought I recognized him. I liked him. What happened? Why is he walking dogs?

THE WOMAN

From what I heard, he refused to report some false information about Covid medicine.

THE MAN

Why would they get rid of him for doing the right thing? That doesn't make any sense.

THE WOMAN

Apparently they were Trump supporters and they were pushing what he said worked, even though the FDA said it wasn't any good, maybe even dangerous.

THE MAN

(Thinking) Damn, she takes a shot at Trump any time she can.

THE WOMAN

This isn't about Trump, it's about station management trying to dictate coverage. That's wrong. What's-his-name was a serious journalist. That's why we watched his news.

THE MAN

Maybe he'll land on his feet.

THE WOMAN

He seems to be having a good time what he's doing.

THE WOMAN

(Thinking) He should sue the station from six ways to Sunday for wrongful termination.

BRETT

(Smiling; quietly) Got a first-rate lawyer on it, lady. Thanks. (Gives a loud whistle) Come on, Bogie. Time for dem bones.

SCENE TWELVE

That evening, Brett is sitting on the front of his desk as his students walk into the classroom, taking smiles and waves from the 15 people who had signed up for his Monterey Peninsula College community seminar, “News Analysis”. At seven o’clock, he gets up off the desk and walks over to close the door. Just as he was doing so he hears a woman’s thoughts.

MISSY

(Thinking) Oh no, oh no, I’m not late! Don’t close the door!

So he doesn’t and instead opens it wide for her. Missy Blaine gives him a big smile of surprise, as if her anxious silent plea has been answered, and she goes to take a seat.

Brett closes the door and comes back to his desk, waiting until everyone is settled.

BRETT

Good evening.

STUDENTS

(The students, all past college age, respond.) Good evening, Mr. Whitson.

BRETT

Tonight we're going to discuss social media and misinformation.

A number of students share looks.

BRETT

What's the difference between news and social media...anyone?

STUDENT ONE

The news is truthful, and social media often isn't.

BRETT

Good. Someone else?

STUDENT TWO

The news is presented by professionals, hopefully journalists, and social media is a mishmash of opinion, gossip, and outright lies.

BRETT

(Laughs) I bet Mark Zuckerberg's name is not at the bottom of your paycheck.

STUDENTS

(Laugh)

BRETT

Why do so many people rely on social media to be, presumably, informed?

STUDENT THREE

Because they want to think themselves informed but they don't want to invest the time and attention to do it right. Plus their family, friends, and whatever are getting informed that way so they are part of a community.

BRETT

Very good, yes. We human beings have a powerful need to affiliate. Being part of a group alleviates fear.

Brett hears Missy's thought.

MISSY

(Thinking) You are a very fine teacher.

BRETT

(He thinks to her) Oh my goodness.

MISSY

(Thinking) You knew you weren't alone.

BRETT

(Thinking) I never communicated this way with anyone...that I know of...awake.

MISSY

(Thinking) We should talk later, if that's all right. I mean, first you have a class to teach.

BRETT

(Thinking) Yes, thank you. (Brett clears his throat and speaks) Do you know people who are informing themselves on social medial, not getting factual information?

Several hands rise, tentatively.

BRETT

No names, but how would you describe them? Do they have any affiliations? Are they political? Do they know they're being misled?

Brett encourages the students to share what they know, pointing to individuals to contribute, nudging them with a specific question. It's an effort to pay attention but he does. He tries not to think about her. He glances at Missy every so often. She's watching him when he does. When the class is over, she is the last to gather her things.

MISSY

(Smiling) Hey Prof, a glass or cup of something?

BRETT

(Smiling back) You already know my answer.

He gathers his things together, and gestures for her to walk out the door. He turns off the lights and follows.

SCENE THIRTEEN

Missy and Brett are sitting at a quiet table in Monterey Tides bar; drinks are on the table.)

MISSY

(Missy leans toward Brett and keeps her voice low.) I was asked to up-brief you.

BRETT

Up-brief me? I feel like I'm just learning to stand up, let alone how to walk.

MISSY

Cute. Okay, we think you are a key player because of your talent and your visibility in this market.

BRETT

That's counts? It's the 125th largest market in the country.

MISSY

Yes, but people recognize you easily because you

have a presenter presence.

BRETT

(Rolls his eyes) Plus I'm not on the air anymore... having been fired.

MISSY

Let go of the theatrics, will you? This is a big deal. We know all that. Now button it and let me 'splain on you.

BRETT

The floor is yours, and by the way, I'm glad that they sent you.

MISSY

Why is that?

BRETT

Because you've obviously got my number.

MISSY

(Reddens slightly, clears her throat, sighs) Yes, well...Okay, you already have discovered that you can hear people's thoughts. And those of your dog friend. What you also need to know is that no one can hear your thoughts unless you want them to. I think Ariel explained this to you, but it is important that you get it. It will make dealing with others much easier. So, you can block everyone you don't know as a baseline, and only let others hear you by granting specific permission. You do that in your own thoughts. You want someone to be able to hear your thoughts, and it's done.

(Brett blinks twice.)

MISSY

Yes. Very good. You had everyone closed out and you just let me in. Good.

BRETT

It's not high tech, is it? Oops, sorry, go ahead.

MISSY

(Smiles warmly, appreciating his understanding, then back to business.) We want to put you back on the air at your station as soon as possible and we know how to do it.

Brett wants to speak but doesn't.

MISSY

We have some of the finest lawyers in the country with us, and two of them have come down from San Francisco to make this happen. First of all, they are filing for an emergency injunction to have your case heard, based on the fact that your reputation as a journalist is such an important part of your career and income. They will say that in the next 40 years you should make something like $150 million as an anchorman; most of it, of course, in a major market and then at a network. They can explain their numbers to you but not to worry, they know this arena very well.

BRETT

I'll pay for your drinks tonight. (Makes a move with his fingers as though he is zipping his lips.)

MISSY

Right. The way they are going to win this is that they have had several phone conversations with the local yokel lawyers that the station hired and learned everything they know about the applicable laws, their strategies, as well as all the coaching they've gotten from the station's home office attorneys in Ohio. Plus they listened to some of their thoughts. I was told they didn't know how they passed the bar.

Brett whistles

MISSY

No, it isn't particularly legal but it isn't illegal because there are no regulations about listening to someone's thoughts. (Pause) Yes, very neat.

BRETT

Would you like something to eat, too?

MISSY

Later. So knowing all of this, they will be able to go before a judge and devastate the station's attorneys' case. They will leave no room for appeal. They will ask the judge to penalize the station for the back pay for the time you missed plus $100,000. They will show their willingness to compromise by coming down to $50,000. The judge will have you back at your anchor desk tomorrow night. (Smiles) Yes, holy moly indeed. (Smiles again) Yes, you can hear my thoughts, but wait until the next time. I don't want to be conflicted, er-hem, until I've told you what else you should know.

BRETT

(Smiles) Are you sure you can keep me out? That's very nice.

MISSY

Oh, lord. I figured there might be leakage if mutual emotions were involved.

BRETT

Yum.

MISSY

Okay, please just try to listen with your ears for a few minutes longer, and then I'm starved. We can have some fun.

BRETT

Let's order first, you can fill me in on the rest I need to know tonight, and then the food will arrive.

He signals the waiter. They order.

BRETT

(In response to her order) You are hungry.

MISSY

(She opens her eyes wide and then her smile widens.) One of the reasons why you are so important, Brett, is that you have such a clear mind when it comes to understanding the state of the world today, especially our country. There's so much screwed up, and now that the vaccinated people with the high CQ are moving into a superior – controlling – position, a lot can be accomplished.

BRETT

I've joked that if I had complete control, I could fix everything by lunch tomorrow...

MISSY

"And it would be an early lunch." Yes, I heard that. Very funny, but it's also realistic to make big changes by listening in on the people who are holding us back, and using their posturing to debunk their positions and proffer far more palatable alternatives.

BRETT

Can this be done in time? I mean, with climate change, Covid, overpopulation, autocrats like Xi, Putin, Bolsonaro, and the rest of their ilk?

MISSY

Climate change is going to take some time to roll back, but the Covid variant is going to dramatically reduce populations, particularly in the overpopulated parts of the southern hemisphere. And there are indications that a new pandemic is spreading that no one realizes yet. That one has to do with fertilization. Birth rates are going to tumble. (Sighs) As far as the dictators are concerned, we anticipate that it won't take long with the revelations of their failed policies based on benefitting the mega-rich and the politicians they've supported, their support will decline dramatically and quickly.

BRETT

(Nods his head.) It certainly sounds preferable to where we are today on the steep downslope. And even plausible. The information can produce the necessary majorities.

MISSY

That's our expectation.

BRETT

(Cocks his head.) So who is "we"? Is there an organization, a cult, a corporation?

MISSY

(Poses a very genuine smile.) No. That's the most fascinating aspect of all this, and yet it makes perfect sense. There is no organization because there is no need for one. The people who were clear-minded enough to know to get their vaccinations, out of practicality and purpose rather than following a leader or out of fear, acted on a higher level of integrity than the overall population. Then those with a significantly elevated consciousness discovered their ability to hear the thoughts of other people and understood that this evolutionary shift was on the level of the fish climbing out of the water onto the sand.

BRETT

(Nods his agreement) Only it was human, global, immediate, and worldwide. It vaulted them to an understanding of what was happening and what it meant. That it was happening on such a scope that they would know what they needed to know and do in conjunction with all the others. Questions were answered before they were fully asked.

MISSY

That's right. Everyone knew what they needed to know and that more knowledge would come to them as needed. That's because we are at a stage where, how do they say it, they were of god and they are god.

BRETT

So there was no hierarchy. No need for challenged leadership. That's the big holy moly.

MISSY

(Laughs)

BRETT

(Looks closely at her) That's the first time I've heard you laugh, Missy. What a lovely sound.

Missy reaches over to Brett, her palm open, and

he gently puts his hand on top of hers.

BRETT

So we get to be together.

They sit silently, listening to each other's thoughts; sighing, smiling. Until the food arrives. They eat. It being close to closing, the waiter returns in a few minutes with the check.

WAITER

No rush folks. Thank you. (Leaves)

He has put the check on the table between them. Missy, snatches it away as Brett is reaching for it.

MISSY

That's for me.

BRETT

What? No.

MISSY

I've got a real job. You're just a teacher.

They both laugh. She puts her credit card on the check and pushes it to the edge of the table.

MISSY

Do you see the guy at the end of the bar?

BRETT

The one who has been looking at you and pretending not to?

MISSY

(Nods) He arrived minutes after we did.

BRETT

Gracious me, is he a husband you didn't tell me about...just when my mind was filling with possibilities?

MISSY

I heard some of those possibilities, Mr. Whitson, but no, I'm not married. I haven't been since... (jokingly she looks at her watch)...six months ago. It was an acrimonious split. He alleged that I was cheating on him.

BRETT

(Surprised at the ex) You wouldn't do that.

MISSY

Only in my thoughts, and no, he wasn't even conscious enough to get vaccinated. Wasn't a fit.

BRETT

Do you know who the guy is then?

MISSY

Not his name, but this isn't the first time I've seen him. I think he's someone my ex hired to follow me, though why he would do that I don't know

The waiter returns with the credit card and receipt to tip and sign. Missy takes care of business.

BRETT

Could you hear what he was thinking, or is he too far away?

MISSY

More like there's too much noise in the room.

BRETT

Does he know you've seen him?

MISSY

Good question. I don't think so. I've not looked at him directly, tonight or before. (Conspiratorial) Women know from an early age about how to deal with such men.

BRETT

Ahso, no wonder I had so much trouble catching their eyes, and probably from that same early age.

MISSY

(Suddenly quiet and gratified) Brett, we are so on the same page. (Big sigh)

BRETT

(Replies with a long appreciative look.) So what do you want to do about the dick? (Clears his throat) I meant the private dick. You know...

MISSY

Yes, a detective. But probably the less polite meaning as well.

BRETT

(Smiling, nodding) Same page indeed. Do you want me to kneel down behind him and you can give him a push?

MISSY

(Shakes her head.) Too many witnesses.

BRETT

There's that. (Thinks) Why don't we get our coats on. I'll go over to the door and wait for you while you go to the ladies' room? I'll see what I can hear him thinking.

MISSY

Very smart.

The waiter returns for the receipt.

WAITER

Thank you, folks. (He walks away and they hear his thought.) Nice tip!

Brett helps Missy on with her coat, slowly and tactilely.

BRETT

Missy, you feel so good.

MISSY

So do you. Take your time.

Missy walks toward the restrooms and Brett over toward the door, seeming to ignore the dick.

SCENE FOURTEEN

Missy and Brett are in her car driving back to the school lot where Brett's car was left.

MISSY

Did our plan work?

BRETT

I heard him think "Zack's not gonna love this." I presume that name means something to you.

MISSY

(Frowns) Yes, Zack's the ex but what did the dick see that made him think Zack wouldn't love it. I mean, so what if we were clearly, um, what?

BRETT

An item?

MISSY

Good. Yes, an item. Did he think I was going into a nunnery?

BRETT

That would have been a crime.

MISSY

You say all of the right things.

BRETT

And since we never even met before a few hours ago, and you cut the cord six months ago...I can appreciate your wondering why the private dick.

MISSY

Was there anything else?

BRETT

(Warm smile) As a matter of fact, there was one thing, before he turned to watch the tball game.

MISSY

(Looks quickly at Brett and sees his smile before returning her eyes to the road.) Yes?

BRETT

I think I'm quoting now. He thought, "What a dickhead to let that babe go."(Pauses to let her enjoy the line) And Missy, I had to catch myself as I was about to tell him, "No kidding, you dick."

MISSY

(Laughs heartily) Oh, that's perfect.

BRETT

I thought so.

They drive into the college parking lot and Missy notices in the rearview mirror the headlights of a car that pulls up on the side of the road before the entrance to the lot. There its lights are turned off. Her tension is palpable.

BRETT

What is it, sweetheart?

A smile appears briefly at the word and fades to what she's seen.

MISSY

A car stopped by the entrance to the parking lot. I wonder if he followed us. He turned his lights off.

Brett is suddenly all action. He pulls out his phone and taps in a number. The call is immediately answered.

BRETT

Hi, Silky, Brett Whitson. What are you doing on the desk at night? (Listens) That may be a good thing that I've got you. Here's the situation. A friend of mine thinks we were followed from the Monterey Tide to the MPC parking lot where my car is parked. He may be following her, and I don't want to leave her alone in case he's dangerous. (Listens) It's probably something benign. She's seen him before and thinks her ex might be up to something, but they were divorced six months ago. (Listens) No, it wasn't nice but he was at fault, not she. (Listens) Oh, could you? That would be great. We'll stay in the parking lot, engine running, lights on, and I'll stay on the phone. (Listens) Great. Thank you.

He reaches over and takes her hand, giving it a light squeeze.

BRETT

He's putting someone on the desk and coming over himself.

MISSY

Silky?

BRETT

Oh, yeah. Eddie Silkwood. He's a Monterey Police lieutenant. Very good man and a friend. I'll tell you about him another time. But he's just the person to find out what's going on. (Sound from the phone) Right. We'll stay until you tell us what to do. (Takes a deep breath.) He'll be in radio contact with the desk, and a patrolman will stay on the line with us.

MISSY

(Shakes her head.) Oh, Brett, I hope I haven't started a tempest in teapot, as they say.

BRETT

Sweetheart, I hope it's nothing more than that but you have every right to find out what that guy is all about.

MISSY

But it may just be a coincidence. Maybe it's someone else who pulled over to the side of the ride.

BRETT

That would be fine with me, but considering that you've seen him before and what I heard him thinking, as it were, we need to find out what's going on with your ex. And make him understand that he's out of your life.

MISSY

Oh, darling... (Tears start to flow, illuminated in the dashboard light. She sniffs and then giggles)

BRETT

What's funny?

MISSY

Our teacher-student relationship.

They both laugh.

Missy's eyes go to her rearview mirror.

MISSY

A police car just pulled up behind him.

Brett turns around and watches as the flashing lights illuminate the parked car in front of it. They sit and watch as the picture remains static.

MISSY

What is your friend doing?

BRETT

He's likely called in for an ID on the car. That can take a minute or two. Then maybe they'll pull the ID of the car owner. Find out if he's a private dick.

They watch as the officer gets out of the police car and walks up to the car in front. He stops at the driver's window where he speaks to the driver and then examines his registration and driver's license. In another minute or so, the officer steps back and the car's lights come on.

The officer returns to his car and turns off his flashing lights. The other car drives away. The police car drives into the parking lot and up to Missy's car. Brett gets out and walks around to the other side of car, opens Missy's door for her and giving her his hand to help her out.

BRETT

I don't know what the story is, Silky, but I am very grateful that I could call and you were there. Especially for Missy Blaine. Missy, this is Lieutenant Edward Silkwood.

SILKWOOD

A pleasure to meet you, Ms. Blaine.

MISSY

(Smiling) The pleasure is certainly all mine, Lieutenant. I had no idea what was going on.

SILKWOOD

(Nods his head) Not knowing is the worst, but let me assure you that you were never in any danger.

Missy puts her arms around Brett, and he holds her.

BRETT

What's the story?

SILKWOOD

It did have to do with your ex, Ms. Blaine. He hired this private dick to follow you to see if you were spending more money than he thought you were supposed to have; according to the divorce, I guess. Maybe to notice that you were with a man though that wasn't primary. The guy said he didn't know what your ex thought was going on, but from what he'd seen, you weren't spending a lot, and not extravagantly. (Clears his throat) He also said he thought your ex was a, um, idiot for letting you get away. Oh, and he apologized for making you nervous. It was just a job, he said, and from what he told me, that was truly all it was for him. Nothing for you to worry about. I would suggest you talk with an attorney tomorrow, probably the one who handled your divorce, and have him contact your ex's attorney. I think this should all go away very quickly.

MISSY

Thank you, Lieutenant Silkwood. I will take care of this promptly. I feel safe again now.

BRETT

Let me add my heartfelt gratitude, Silky.

SILKWOOD

Glad to be of assistance, my friend, and you, Ms. Blaine. Have a nice evening.

SCENE FIFTEEN

Fifteen minutes later, Missy and Brett are in her kitchen. She's making coffee.

MISSY

Thank you for following me home, dear Brett. I hope I didn't sound paranoid, especially with what we learned from your policeman friend. That there was nothing to worry about from Detective Dick.

They laugh.

BRETT

No need to worry about your ex, but we can find out what that's all about. And by the way, I'm glad that you invited me in, Missy. It didn't feel like the evening was ready to end.

MISSY

It didn't, did it? What's going on? We're acting like love-struck teenagers.

BRETT

Feels good, doesn't it?

MISSY

(Sternly) This must be a constant for a handsome television anchorman.

BRETT

(Posing angst) It's exhausting. They chase me down the aisles of the supermarket.

MISSY

(Serious, smiling) How did this happen? Was it arranged by the universe? Are we supposed to be a team to save the world?

BRETT

That must be it.

MISSY

And the personal relationship is a perk.

BRETT

Such a deal.

Facing no resistance, he pulls her toward him and into his arms. For a moment they look into each other's eyes and then they kiss.

SCENE SIXTEEN

Midmorning the nest day. Brett is walking into his house. The landline phone across the room is ringing. He smiles at it but ignores it. He sheds his coat and takes out his cellphone.

BRETT

Oops.

It was off. He turns it on. He waits, looking off into the distance of his recent past. Sighs. The cellphone dings that it's on. He pushes some buttons and then scans a list. He shrugs, then walks into his office, puts the cellphone on his desk, and walks out and down the hall to the bathroom. Looks in the mirror at his stubbly face.

BRETT

If you're going to be anchoring the news tonight, you need to clean up.

He turns on the shower and starts to take off his clothes.

SCENE SEVENTEEN

Bright-eyed and bushy-tailed, Missy is sitting at a table on her patio. She's on the phone.

MISSY

Thank you, Murph. I didn't think it was anything serious. Nothing you couldn't straighten out. I feel sorry for the guy, but the judge said he was out of my life, and I want to make sure he's not coming back. Be well.

She disconnects the call, looking very satisfied. She picks up the phone to call Brett but stops, smiles, and puts the phone down. She sits back in her chair, closes her eyes, slows her breathing, concentrating and relaxing at the same time. After a short time, a bright smile blossoms on her face. After a few moments, she picks up the phone to note the time, and puts it back down on the table. She remains the way she is, occasionally nodding her head, her face expressing various feelings, all positive.

SCENE EIGHTEEN

Brett and Missy are sitting at a table in a nice restaurant. Having just ordered their lunch, he hands their menus to the waitress with a "Thank you"

BRETT

Thank you for coming over to Salinas. I was going to invite you to my place, but I was afraid I'd never get to the office.

MISSY

Oh, yes, and on this re-launch of your anchor-dom.

BRETT

If it weren't for how I might leverage the job into bigger and better things...

MISSY

And $150 million.

BRETT

Aw, peanuts, but I might find a career less time-consuming, less public, and in some sort of working partnership with you.

MISSY

You mean, like what we're doing...saving the world?

BRETT

Something like that.

Missy starts to reach her hand across the table to his but catches herself.

MISSY

That connection we had this morning...between our houses...What is that five, six miles?

BRETT

Something like that. I guess it's not a matter of distance that we can do that but the intensity of the thoughts, and of the mutual intention.

Missy shakes her head, smiling.

MISSY

Frickin' amazing.

BRETT

That's an understatement.

MISSY

Uh-huh, about everything. And I will add wonderful. (Shifts in her chair and the topic.) How was the call from the station this morning?

BRETT

Hah. I had forgotten to turn my phone on this morning until I got home.

MISSY

You were otherwise distracted, methinks.

BRETT

Wethinks. Anyway, it wasn't the local station, but someone from corporate out in Ohio called at eleven his time, expecting it wasn't too earlier for me, but I didn't get the message until after ten. I returned the call. He sounded a little annoyed but he let it pass. I mean, what was the point. He went over the agreement, delivered the typical "glad to have you back in the game" palaver. I told him I was looking forward to getting back to work, for myself and the station.

MISSY

So much business talk, especially when lawyers

are involved, is just a dance.

BRETT

Hmm. I ran across a quote the other day that speaks to that: "Debate is the death of conversation."

MISSY

Who said that?

BRETT

Someone I didn't know. Emil Ludwig.

MISSY

He certainly got that right. But those who are reading each other's thoughts, there's a presumption of telling the truth, so there's no need to debate, just to converse.

BRETT

Yes. I like that.

MISSY

Brett, I'm so glad that you're only doing the six o'clock news and not the late news at eleven.

BRETT

Whoever thought to put that into the new agreement, we owe a very nice bottle of something.

The waitress arrives and puts their meals on the table. Thanked and their needing nothing else at the moment, she departs. They dig into their lunches. They share thoughts non-verbally.

BRETT

Missy, do you have any sense about how this will all turn out? I don't mean about us. I've never felt so sure of anything in my life as I do about our being together.

MISSY

You mean our day job.

BRETT

That's it.

They chuckle.

MISSY

Hmm. I hadn't thought about it, but thinking about it now, I think it somehow will make progress. Despite all the mishegoss – the corruption, ignorance, and insanity – I come back to us being extraordinary creatures. Mostly we take notice of it in sports. I'm not a sports nut, but this made the news. A clip of some basketball player scoring 49 points in a game. It just seemed so incredible that he made so many shots, and of course with the players from the other team trying to stop him.

BRETT

I saw that, too. Astounding. I remember way back when, watching Johnny Miller, the golfer, putting. That ball must have crossed three state lines, up and down hills, hither and yon, and it went right into the cup, I think from 30 feet away.

MISSY

That's right, and if our minds can produce such sensational events, we should surely be able to apply ourselves to pioneer solutions to get the planet spinning the way we want it to.

BRETT

Applying ourselves on new paths of creativity, with our hearts supporting with trust and knowledge.

SCENE NINETEEN

Early evening. Missy and Brett are walking on the street above the beach.

MISSY

How was it to be back at your desk?

BRETT

It was fine. I could tell that the people at the station were watching me more closely, which was to be expected, but I felt so comfortable in my skin – your arrival in my life being the obvious reason – that they felt everything was all right. Maybe not quite the same, but all right.

MISSY

I thought your opening was very smart.

BRETT

(Repeats it) Good evening, I'm Brett Whitson, and it's good to be back with you to keep you informed on our world, our country, and our community. And then I went on with the news.

MISSY

It sounded like that wasn't scripted.

BRETT

It wasn't, except in my mind.

MISSY

Did management know that you would say something?

BRETT

We never talked about it. But something had to be said since there was such a public break-up.

MISSY

Well, what you said and how you said it was the height of professionalism.

BRETT

Why thank you.

MISSY

And I think it underscores why you are the right person for whatever it is we are doing, what we are supposed to achieve.

BRETT

It does feel right, Missy. Different and right. And only being with you makes more sense.

MISSY

You got that right, buster. (She nudges him) And you don't have to choose between it and us.

<u>*SCENE TWENTY*</u>

The next morning. The sign on the small but classy office building lists among the three tenants “Blaine Consulting”. (Dissolve to Missy’s office.) She’s standing behind her desk. Her well-dressed client, with whom she’s just finished a session, is standing across from her and bidding good-bye.

MISSY

I think what you are doing is simply wonderful, for you, your employees - excuse me, co-workers - and the stockholders. You are proving that high consciousness values translate into growth in earnings.

CLIENT

You started us on this road, Missy, and we are all grateful. See you in a couple of weeks at the annual.

MISSY

Yes, looking forward to it. (Her client turns for

the door.) Oh, you said you got your vaccinations, didn't you?

CLIENT

Of course. It was required of everyone in the office.

MISSY

Any hesitation?

CLIENT

One woman needed a little convincing because she was thinking of getting pregnant but she was shown the facts and was right on board.

MISSY

Good for you. Thanks.

The client waves good-bye from the doorway. Missy sits back down, a thoughtful look on her face. After a few moments, she punches in two numbers on her intercom phone. Franklin answers.

FRANKLIN

Yo, boss lady.

MISSY

Yo, brilliant numbers guy, do you have anything on what companies, organizations, geographic affinities have high levels of consciousness and have gotten their vaccinations? (There is a long silence.) Are you still there?

Her office door opens and Franklin enters, sitting in the chair in front of her desk, his laptop in his lap.

FRANKLIN

No, I'm here.

MISSY

Always a pleasure to see you, Franklin, but your sudden appearance –

FRANKLIN

...From the middle of our phone call.

MISSY

Certainly raises its own questions.

FRANKLIN

(Pointing down at his laptop.) And I have some answers for you.

MISSY

How, may I ask, is it that there is this synchronistic serendipitous coincidence?

FRANKLIN

You know what Einstein said about coincidence?

MISSY

Actually I do. He said, "Coincidence is God's way of remaining anonymous." A favorite quote of mine. Why did you have the data I was asking for at your fingertips?

FRANKLIN

Of course that's my job to serve you, but... (He twisted his head to make sure the door was closed and no one else was in the room) ...I think you already know. You must know. It's about the people of high CQ who have gotten their jabs. (Thinking) And they – all of us – can hear people's thoughts. Those who are on the same plane, so to say.

MISSY

(Thinking) How did you find out?

Franklin shakes his head as if to clear it and they are back to using their voices again.

FRANKLIN

It was crazy. I thought I had dreamed it, but while I was having it and afterwards, it seemed really real. And I think it was.

MISSY

What was the dream?

FRANKLIN

(Takes a deep breath and lets it out) I was in a place which was mostly colorless. There were a lot of puffy clouds.

MISSY

Sort of like how heaven might be in a movie?

FRANKLIN

Yes, yes...that's what I thought it was. Like *Heaven Can Wait* with Warren Beatty. Yeah, but he didn't die.

MISSY

Anyway...

FRANKLIN

Anyway – how did you know that? (Pauses; no answer) Anyway, in the dream I have a conversation with a guy only our lips aren't moving, and he tells me what's going on. What you asked me for, about the higher conscious people who had been vaccinated. He said a lot of those people were discovering that they could read people's thoughts. Or rather, hear what they were thinking.

MISSY

When did this happen, Franklin?

FRANKLIN

A coupla nights ago. (Peers at her.) You must have had this dream or whatever it is, too.

MISSY

(Looks hard at him) You are not to share this information with anyone. Is that clear? The research you will be doing on the subject and our conversations.

FRANKLIN

Sure. I wonder how many people have found out about this. Can hear people's thoughts.

MISSY

That's what we need to track. Who they are, what distinguishes them, where are they. Everything; every bit of data. Also any information sources on the subject, any news outlets that might report on it.

FRANKLIN

(Typing notes into his laptop.) Right. (Looks up at her.) Is there anyone here at the office who knows about this?

MISSY

I would like to know that, too. Can you stay on top of this? Do you need any help on it?

FRANKLIN

I'd have to share what you are interested in.

MISSY

Not until we know she or he is part of the plot. Oh, and speaking of plot, I'd like to know what you find out about any opposition.

FRANKLIN

(Points down at his laptop again) Yup. Got that already.

MISSY

May I ask, do you know anyone outside of us...

FRANKLIN

Who's part of the plot? (She nods her head) No. Not even suspicions. But you work me so hard, I don't have a social life to speak of.

MISSY

(Feigning patience; smiling) And...?

FRANKLIN

Well, there's not a lot of information but some of

it is interesting to the point of significant, for we're starting at ground zero. First, what I'm seeing, what little there is, has surfaced in the first 48 hours. (She nods) Second, no one, and I mean no one who is saying anything about this is a political leader. Also, everything that I've seen seems to have come from quiet, tentative voices. No trumpeting. More respectful, curious, interested.

MISSY

Wow. That's big.

FRANKLIN

Yes it is. No one is crowing. I never saw that on a breaking story.

MISSY

Any patterns yet?

FRANKLIN

Educated, formally or otherwise. Thoughtful. Not selling, more like feeling out.

MISSY

Makes sense.

FRANKLIN

Mostly white, at least middle class for the most

part. Northeast coast, West Coast mostly central California to up north, some college towns, sprinkling around the big cities as you'd expect.

MISSY

Religious? Political? Cults?

FRANKLIN

Evangelicals are very low numbers, of course; also Ultra-orthodox Jews and Muslims. They prefer to shun responsibility and keep god external. Very few Republicans. No existing cults that I can see, and no new cults have formed, at least not yet.

MISSY

Are there any definitive media that they monitor?

FRANKLIN

Through which they might be reached or would coalesce? Nothing yet but again it's pretty soon.

MISSY

Understandable, yes. They have to figure out what's going on first inside themselves, wonder why they have been "chosen", who they might discuss it with, et cetera, et cetera. (Adds) Anything about age? Children?

FRANKLIN

Hold a sec. (He types.) Hmm. Maybe a bell curve on the age question, but again very thin. Twenty-five to forty is the largest cluster. And maybe more than I would have guessed in the mid-fifties.

MISSY

That makes sense, with the younger people finding they will have to be dealing with life in a new way and the older group wondering if they should be re-examining where they are.

FRANKLIN

Uh-huh. Sounds right.

MISSY

Good, Franklin. Stay on top of this. Get me summaries when you come in in the morning, lunch time, and when you're leaving the office. And if you get anything new off hours, please send it to me on that super-encrypted line.

FRANKLIN

Will do, Missy.

MISSY

Yes, it's grown-up time.

SCENE TWENTY-ONE

Missy and Brett go for an early lunch that day at Tarpy's, before he had to get to the station. They sat next to each other, rather than across, but only if someone was paying attention would get a hint of their closeness. There was no kissing and minimal touching, above the level of the table. Missy had excused herself to make a call outside the restaurant. Brett was sitting quietly when Spiff Jerkins, the Channel Eight station vice president, stumbled up to the table, clearly in his cups. Brett was immediately on alert.

JERKINS

(Voice is loud and slurred) You got me into trouble, you sonovabitch.

Brett says nothing, but he sees that the man has caught the attention of several waiters and the few patrons in the restaurant at that the opening hour.

JERKINS

Whaddya say to that, you sonovabitch?

BRETT

I didn't do anything to get you into trouble, Spiff. I didn't even know the company was going to bring me back until last week.

JERKINS

That's a lot of BS. You made a whole big stink and threatened them.

BRETT

That's simply not the truth. I didn't threaten anyone. I didn't even ask for the job back.

JERKINS

You're lying. You're a liar.

The manager comes up to Jerkins and speaks quietly to him.

MANAGER

Sir, could I ask you to please lower your voice?

JERKINS

(Turns to the manager, predictably raises his voice.) I don't have to be quiet. You're a sonova-bitch, too.

MANAGER

Sir, then I'm going to have to ask you to please leave.

Jerkins gives the manager a shove, knocking him onto a table which crashes to the floor. He orders a waiter.

Call the Police.

MISSY

(Returning to the scene; shouts) He's got a gun!

Jerkins spins around to face her. Brett pushes their table over into Jerkins, knocking him to the ground. He steps around the mess, slams Jerkin's head against the floor, and pulls his wrists together behind his back.

MISSY

(Thinks to him) The gun is in his right back pocket.

BRETT

(Thinks back to her) Please get it and put it in my coat pocket.

She pulls the gun out of the man's pocket and puts it in Brett's pocket.

BRETT

(Aloud) Good. (To the assistant manager) Call the police. And is there a rope? Or can you take off his necktie?

The assistant manager quickly pulls off his tie

and hands it to Missy.

MISSY

Will this work?

BRETT

(Takes the tie) Yes. He's still woozy and the police will be here in minutes.

He double-ties the man's wrists together, checks to make sure they will hold, and stands up. As if on cue, sirens can be heard. Missy moves close to him.

BRETT

(very quietly.) You were - are - wonderful. (Looks around again; no one is close enough to hear him.) I presume you also heard him thinking about the gun. And he must have been startled when he heard that you saw it. When the police ask you how you knew, say you saw the outline of it in his pants pocket when he pushed the manager.

Missy gives him a short nod.

Brett pulls out his phone and punches in the direct line to call the station's news director.

BRETT

It's Brett, I need McCarthy. Urgent.

NEWS DESK PERSON

Brett, he's in a meeting.

BRETT

I said urgent. Get him on the phone NOW.

The desk person puts the phone down and goes to closed door of the news director's office where she still knocks tentatively.

MCCARTHY

(Through the door; annoyed) I'm busy.

NEWS DESK PERSON

(Opens the door) It's Brett. Says it's urgent.

MCCARTHY

(Picks up the phone) Couldn't this wait? I'm in a meeting.

BRETT

Only if you want Channel Five to beat the pants off us reporting that Spiff Jerkins was arrested for assault and carrying a gun.

MCCARTHY

(Shouts) What!?! Holy Sh...

BRETT

Send the closet crew and a reporter to Tarpy's

ASAP. (Clicks off) (To Missy) I can't stand amateurs.

SCENE TWENTY-TWO

At the Channel Eight studios, Brett is in the anchor chair.

BRETT

And finally tonight, this story...that we regret having to report as it involves an official at Channel Eight. Suzi Oh has that story.

VIDEO REPORT

(Suzi Oh voice-over appropriate visuals) Shortly after eleven this morning, at Tarpy's restaurant off Highway 68 in Monterey, Spiff Jerkins, vice president of Channel Eight, got into an argument with our own anchorman, Brett Whitson. He alleged that Whitson has caused damage to his standing with First California Media, the company that owns this station. It appeared that Mr. Jerkins might have been under the influence of some substance as he was unsteady on his feet and slurring his words. When he refused to lower his voice, he was asked to leave by the restaurant manager. Mr. Jerkins then gave the manager a push, knocking him onto and breaking a nearby table. Another customer then said that Mr. Jerkins had a gun, which she had seen in his pocket when he shoved the manager. At that point, Mr. Whitson shoved the table behind which he was sitting at Mr. Jenkins, knocking him to the floor. Mr. Whitson then tackled and restrained Mr. Jenkins, tying his hands behind his back, and pocketing his gun until the police arrived. They arrested Mr. Jerkins, and it was expected that he will be charged regarding the assault of the restaurant manager and having a firearm without a permit. Hobart Lipscomb, the president of Channel Eight had this to say: "All of us at Channel Eight are deeply saddened by this unfortunate event. We are relieved that the manager of the restaurant suffered no serious injuries. And we are grateful that Mr. Whitson was able to quickly defuse the situation without further injury to others." Mr. Lipscomb said there would be no further comment at this time regarding Mr. Jerkins future with the station or the company. Suzi Oh, Channel Eight News, at Tarpy's in Monterey.

BRETT

(On camera) Thank you, Suzi Oh, for covering

that story. That duty fell to her rather than me because I was a participant, and it would have been inappropriate for me as a journalist to report on the matter. But I can add these comments. First, I said and did nothing to undermine Spiff Jerkins position with the company. I had no reason to and would never have attacked him or any of my colleagues here. Along with the rest of the staff here at Channel Eight, I wish him well in dealing with the issues that brought on this situation. That's the Channel Eight evening news. Tune in at eleven for the latest news. I'm Brett Whitson.

SCENE TWENTY-THREE

Brett is at his home office.

LESLIE

(Calling from her car) OMG, Brett, you don't mess around, do you?

BRETT

Good morning, Leslie.

LESLIE

I can only imagine that it was worse than what was reported on your station last night. You weren't hurt, were you? You didn't look bad. No black eyes, large bandages, blood on your clothes.

BRETT

No, I was fine.

LESLIE

Anything juicy that wasn't in the report?

BRETT

No, nothing juicy. They would have liked not to mention the stumbling around and the slurring, but I pointed out to the station chief that it wouldn't have made sense that he shoved the manager. No one sober would have done that.

LESLIE

Lipscomb didn't look very happy.

BRETT

Of course not. He and Jerkins were responsible for the mess in the first place. Lipscomb hurt himself by firing me and costing the company a lot of money. Jerkins just added salt to his wound.

LESLIE

And you, my friend, you're still feeling wonderful?

BRETT

Never better...truly never better.

LESLIE

I believe you. So what's your mystery potion? You think it's the vaccinations?

BRETT

(Mimicking the commercial) "Try it, you'll like it."

LESLIE

(Unhappy) Yeah.

BRETT

(Sympathetic) Did you talk about it with Gladys?

LESLIE

Yes, we talked about it. She isn't budging.

BRETT

She's not a budger.

LESLIE

(Sighs loudly) No, she's not.

BRETT

And that's a problem for you.

LESLIE

(Sardonic chuckle) And you're the shrink now?

BRETT

(Sincere) I know it's been difficult for you.

LESLIE

Yeah. Thanks.

BRETT

You haven't been happy lately, at least when I've seen you or we talked on the phone. And you have a right to be. (Pause) Maybe you need to take a break.

LESLIE

We talked about that the other day.

BRETT

And?

LESLIE

She got all defensive.

BRETT

So she can't be very happy either. (Pause) How long have you been together?

LESLIE

Seventeen months.

BRETT

How's Bogie doing with it?

LESLIE

He's not happy either, except when he's coming to see you.

BRETT

I have a suggestion...two actually.

LESLIE

Uh-oh.

BRETT

Yes. The first is for you to let me have Bogie for a weekend. I'm home at seven tonight, and I don't go back in until Monday noonish.

LESLIE

Maybe. And?

BRETT

Get yourself vaccinated. I guarantee that your life will get better the day you have your second shot.

LESLIE

(Dubious) Yeah, right.

BRETT

(Firmly) Guaranteed, Leslie.

LESLIE

How can you say such a thing?

BRETT

Actually I can.

LESLIE

How?

BRETT

Remember how good I sounded when I got the second shot, and I asked you about aftereffects?

LESLIE

(Cautiously) Yesss.

BRETT

Things have only gotten better. I am at a high point in my life, Leslie. I've never felt better... happier, secure, confident, purposeful, having it all and more.

LESLIE

And you attribute this to the vaccinations?

BRETT

Yes. (Emphasizes) I know it couldn't have happened without the shots.

LESLIE

Why? How do you know?

BRETT

I can't tell you.

LESLIE

Why not?

BRETT

You wouldn't believe me?

LESLIE

But I would know after I got the shot? You would tell me?

BRETT

You would know and I could confirm what you know.

LESLIE

You're not one to play games with me, Brett. What's this all about?

BRETT

My dear friend, you can't understand until you've had the second shot. (Chuckles) It's kinda like when you lose your virginity. Life changes for you.

SCENE TWENTY-FOUR

Brett is in his kitchen. Missy is sitting at the dining table, a glass of wine before her, comfortably rubbing Bogie's head.

MISSY

What a great being.

BRETT

You're picking up his thoughts?

MISSY

(Giggles) Well, he's kinda monosyllabic, but he keeps up his side of the conversation.

Bogie moans.

MISSY

(Missy laughs) See?

BRETT

Yup.

MISSY

So it seems like what you said to Leslie maybe have gotten through. Not just about Bogie, but it sounds like she's going to get vaccinated.

BRETT

I think so.

MISSY

And she'll tell her friend afterwards?

BRETT

Gladys. I think Glad will know. And if she asks Leslie, Leslie will tell her the truth.

MISSY

Would it stop her from getting the second shot?

BRETT

No. I don't see it.

MISSY

Good. She sounds like a valuable part of the plot.

BRETT

"Plot"?

MISSY

Hah. That's how I describe it to Franklin – you

know Franklin, my data whiz – that's the how we the people who have the CQ, gotten the shots, and are experiencing the larger reality.

BRETT

Funny. I suppose those who aren't there yet, and aren't going to be, probably would see it as such. A plot against them.

MISSY

Franklin was talking about some friends he plays pickleball with. They're all vaccinated. Won't even play with people who aren't. One of them was talking about how the red states are seeing their case numbers, hospitalizations, and deaths on the rise. A lot of it may be the Covid variant. While in the blue states the numbers continue to go down. He said none of them expressed any empathy. In fact, there was outright hostility, like those people who didn't get the jabs and got sick should have to pay their own medical bills.

BRETT

I can understand that. I mean, there is virtually no reason not to get the shots, unless you could be injured by them. Otherwise, there is no valid excuse, and not only are people risking their own health but also the people they come in contact with. (Shakes his head) Of course we know all that, but I think there's something serious wrong with the people who come up with an excuse not to. Especially for political or religious reasons.

MISSY

And the antivaxxers, especially.

Bogie growls.

MISSY

I love this dog. (Ruffles his neck) So are Leslie and Glad – Gladys – going to stay together do you think?

BRETT

Dunno. I have known Leslie for a long time. She's bright, caring, funny. A good person. She deserves happiness too.

MISSY

You don't care so much for Gladys?

BRETT

She was never warm with me. I think she hates men.

MISSY

That wouldn't put her at the top of my list.

BRETT

No. I just would like what's best with Leslie. And may Glad get on her best track.

MISSY

Brett, were you as thoughtful before you got your vaccinations?

BRETT

I don't think so. I wasn't mean and thoughtless. I watched movies like *Enchanted April* and *My Dinner with André.* (Laughs) I think that changed for me, too.

MISSY

I've been thinking about it in broader terms. It's all about energy. Not only thinking and hearing thoughts, but being more aware of other people's feelings.

BRETT

I've felt that change, too, Missy. Like with Jerkins. A month ago, it would have been my inclination to stand up to him.

MISSY

And get shot?

BRETT

There's that. Or maybe exactly that.

MISSY

That's where I was going with this. It's like we can see people's auras. Not the colored garland or Kirlian imagery. More subtle than that. Not actually seeing something, with our eyes, but perceiving it.

BRETT

That would make sense. I knew at some level that I needed to deal with Jerkins quietly. I put off an angry confrontation, let the manager step in, and then disabled him without it being a brawl.

MISSY

You were very effective , my dear, and that's how I think we want to rate things. That's what we need, to be effective. So much to get done.

BRETT

Sweetheart, I asked you this the other day. Do you have the sense that this will all work out... for the best? Have you thought about it anymore?

MISSY

You mean, will we live through all of this?

BRETT

Yes.

MISSY

I do, my dear Brett. (Laughs) Does that make it sound like we'll survive and get married?

Brett walks over to Missy. She stands up into his arms. They kiss long and slow. Their mouths part slowly but not very far.

BRETT

I think we are already, darling Missy.

MISSY

And our honeymoon will go on like this forever.

SCENE TWENTY-FIVE

Leslie has driven alone to Brett's house to pick up Bogie. She is sitting with him, Missy, and Brett on the deck. There is some partially consumed food and drink on the table.

LESLIE

(To Missy) When I first heard the change in Brett's tone, I thought it truly was his second vaccination. (Smiles all around) But just this short time I've been with you, I can see that you were the catalyst. I've never seen him so happy, so at peace with himself.

MISSY

How nice of you to say, but now that you've had your second shot, you must know that it had a powerful effect on you. Considering your own situation. What you said about your relationship.

LESLIE

It was significant, surely. I hadn't realized that

Gladys was all out of shape because she was so sensitive to my not being true to myself. When I told her that I had gotten the first shot and was going out to get the second, she was relieved. It was like I had given her permission to say her truth.

BRETT

Do you think she's just taking off some time or is it going to be long term?

LESLIE

(Slight grimace) I think she's going to find herself feeling better on her own.

MISSY

Sounds like it is better for both of you, if that doesn't sound presumptuous.

LESLIE

Not at all. In truth, I'm glad you can feel it.

BRETT

Leslie, I have a question of a professional nature.

LESLIE

Hey, I'm off on Sundays. Call my service to get on the calendar. (Chuckles around; she nods at him)

BRETT

We were talking about the vaccination-consciousness effect. We shared how we all became aware of it, and what is has meant for us. How do you explain it in psychiatric terms?

LESLIE

Well, so much for having Sunday off. (Laughs) I don't think there is enough known yet. No one in the field I've read has had anything major to say about it. Most everyone, and not just psychiatrists, are waiting for more data.

BRETT

But...?

LESLIE

I don't want to sound like a heretic, after all the money I spent getting my degrees, and all the work I've done with my patients, but I think what we're seeing - what we ourselves have experienced personally - is that this is supra-psychiatric, indeed beyond intellectual as well.

BRETT

(To Missy) That's what you were saying, darling. An evolutionary shift of the importance of the amphibians.

LESLIE

(Nods her head thoughtfully toward Missy) I think you're spot on, Dr. Blaine. Maybe I need a new couch. (Laughter)

Brett is deep in thought for a minute; Missy and Leslie see it and remain quiet.

BRETT

Thank you. Here's what I was thinking, if you weren't listening in. (Both shake their heads) I have been wondering what my role is in all of this. Yes, I'm a journalist and have a good presence - (nods to Missy) - but I could never see that it was about my being at Channel Eight. I mean, what could I say during the evening news that would reach a significant and receptive audience. Especially having been fired and even though I was brought back. And then that matter with Jerkins. How could that possibly benefit my reach or image? That's where I was stumped. But it finally got through to me that the role was right but the medium was different. What if I were to produce a news report and whether or not Channel Eight – slash First California Media – put it on the air, I would put it on social media? People pass around videos through Facebook and Twitter like crazy. I think that's all some people do in their waking hours. And some of the videos on YouTube have been watched literally billions of times. Not just for entertainment but actual information.

MISSY

Enlightenment, in fact.

BRETT

Yes. Well, maybe not go that far (Laughter) but to at least put the information before the public to get people vaccinated and maybe wake themselves up. They would do it because the ability to hear the thoughts of other people is a distinguishing power. I have to think a lot of folks would at least start by getting the shots.

LESLIE

Oh Brett, that's perfect for you.

BRETT

(Missy raises her hand) Yes, Ms. Blaine.

MISSY

Give them the information by telling a story. Your story, some of all of our stories. You can engage people more easily and more deeply if they don't have to learn but are there to be engaged in a story.

BRETT

Yes. Exactly right. As McLuhan said, "Anyone who tries to make a distinction between education and entertainment doesn't know the first thing about either."

The three sit down around the table and talk, Brett making notes. Bogie making a number of "yum" sounds.

SCENE TWENTY-SIX

A television news report with Brett on camera and the expected graphics and on-camera interviews.

BRETT

This Channel Eight special comes to you from the station owner, First California Media. It has to do with widespread experiences of a previously unknown side effect a number of recipients of the full vaccination program for protection from Covid-19. Those individuals appear to share an additional trait. They are people who have the less specific but critical quality of higher consciousness. Most of us are familiar with the term IQ, for intelligence quotient. A new term, CQ, stands for consciousness quotient, and the people we are talking about in this report have a higher CQ. What does it mean to have higher consciousness? It means a greater state of being awake and aware of one's surroundings. It means a greater awareness of the mind, how it works, and how it experiences the world.

That may be somewhat confusing. Another way to say it is that people with higher consciousness have a more detailed perception of life around them.

But let's return to the premise of this report. People who have had their full coronavirus vaccination – either the single shot of the Johnson & Johnson or the two shots of the Pfizer or Moderna – and also have a higher consciousness are reporting feeling less anguish, more peace, and a greater sense of being present. They say that they are less scattered in their thinking.

That is significant in itself. They are less fearful, don't feel as pressed in dealing with life's various challenges. But an ever greater factor for these people is that they are also finding that in some situations they are able to hear the thoughts of people around them. Let me say that again. Some people who have been fully inoculated from the coronavirus and who are more conscious are able to hear the thoughts of other people. They can also communicate with people who have been vaccinated and a high-level consciousness, mind to mind, thoughts to thoughts, without speaking aloud. This is an incredible advance in evolution.

To be clear, it wasn't the inoculation itself, it was being aware that being vaccinated was proof of my social conscience and my commitment to participating on an informed level. To demonstrate my determination to protect myself and others from Covid, and to make the community safer.

I can tell you from personal experience that when I received my second Pfizer vaccination, within minutes I started to feel better. More relaxed but more present and aware. I also felt less hurried, which showed in my driving. I didn't drive as fast as I used to. Not that I was aggressive on the road but I didn't feel the same pressure to get to where I was going.

There were other signs of change. I didn't get annoyed as easily as I used to. And I found myself listening more rather than having to jump in with what I had to say. And my thinking was clearer. My mind was open to considering more possibilities. My thinking wasn't as cut and dry; there was more subtlety and nuance...more detail.

I also found that in my conversations with people I knew, I was not taking them for granted. I looked at them every time with a fresh mind. And I was delighted to discover that I was seeing a new person; more thoughtful, more complex, more interesting, more valuable. And in their response to me I could see that they found me more interesting, more fun to be with. The exchanges were so significant that my friends were asking me if everything was all right. That I seemed changed.

The differences were more than noteworthy. I had never experienced myself this way, and I wondered what caused the change. I was certainly aware that it had begun just after my second inoculation. I remembered having a quality conversation with the nurse who gave me the shot. It was not just off-the-cuff, it was substantial. We both valued the exchange for the words and the emotions.

That night I slept as soundly as ever. When I woke up, I remembered a dream that was so vivid I wondered if it was actually a dream. It had to do with my meeting someone and we had a conversation of thoughts. This fellow told me that a number of people who had been fully vaccinated and were particularly conscious would be moving to a higher evolutionary level. Someone later referred to the shift on the level of the fish coming out onto the land. Interestingly, I was not startled by this news. It was that I already knew it, though I hadn't heard anything like this or ever thought about it. He said that other people would be coming into my life with more information, and he said I needn't wonder about who they might be, that I would know.

I decided as a journalist that this needed to be professionally investigated. I spoke with a several people I knew who might shed light on the situation. As it turned out, they had all had been vaccinated and they were all very bright. To be clear, they weren't just smart; they were consciously aware. They had a higher-than-average level of consciousness. And they were all having the same experiences as I was. They felt better than they ever had before, and their minds were operating far more efficiently. They, too, could hear the thoughts of other people.

First was a psychiatrist I'd known many years. When I first asked her about side effects from the vaccinations, she said that I sounded different to her, different enough so that she worried about me. At that point, she hadn't been vaccinated.

LESLIE

I remember his first call. He sounded distant, in a way, and very soft. Not in terms of the volume of his voice, but his personality was less forceful. We spoke again and while he still seemed different, there was a strength in his words that persuaded me that he was fine. Even, as he was saying, better. A month later, after I had gotten both my shots, I knew exactly what he was talking about because it produced the same change in me. I felt more at peace, less assertive, better able to listen. I might add that the changes made me noticeably more effective in my work with my patients. Not to overstate the difference, but it was like my life had been black-&-white and now was in color.

BRETT

Another experience I had was when I was a teaching an evening community class at Monterey Community College. I had gone to close the classroom door to start when suddenly I heard, "Oh no, oh no, I'm not late! Don't close the door!" When I heard her first words, I turned to look and saw that she wasn't speaking. Again, I wasn't really surprised, except that she was a very lovely person who had been in my class for a number of weeks and I had never had this happen before.

MISSY

After the class we met and discussed in detail what we had individually experienced and where we thought this might be going. Most of the time we talked normally, but sometimes we communicated with our thoughts. On one occasion we found that we could do so when we were more than five miles apart. I had a similar first encounter in a dream like Brett's and the same response. I didn't know where this was all going, but it felt like I was following a script that was thoroughly right and appropriate. I didn't have to know what was coming, and I would feel perfectly comfortable with it.

BRETT

One of the people who worked with Missy was a specialist in data collection and analysis. He, too, had had his inoculations and was a highly conscious person. When Missy called him to do custom research on people who had been vaccinated and were conscious, he raced into her office and told her of his experience very much like hers. Then he set about finding what data was available about who was feeling significantly better, who could hear the thoughts of other people, and how were these people different from the general population.

FRANKLIN

The first look, it was pretty skimpy. I mean, so many people didn't know what was going on, and they had no one to talk to about it in the beginning. But even then, the patterns were the same: vaccinated and very conscious. Later, week by week the numbers went up following the same track. While hard numbers are difficult to track down, there are significant movements, particularly in this country but also in Europe, away from religion to a more individualized spiritualism that is about integrity and personal responsibility. That fits with early assessments that consciousness is partly about intellect but mostly about character. So my reading of the numbers is that more like 37% of the country could be deemed of above average consciousness, and probably 80% of them have gotten their shots. Almost a third of the country. Of course, most of them don't know about what's going, or what we're talking about, at least not outside their closest circles of friends or family. That is, if they are talking to anyone, but that will change. Quickly, I think.

BRETT

Let me close with this. None of the people I've talked to about this has viewed it negatively. Why this has happened now, some say, may be due to the feeling that society as we have known seems to have come off the tracks. That fear and confusion is widespread, and Nature has responded by giving a good number of people quieter minds and the ability to reduce fear by knowing what some people are thinking before they act, thereby averting conflict. More people focused on our shared humanity can only help.

Finally, I think more information will be forthcoming in a public way. When it does, we will report it. I'm Brett Whitson for First California Media on Channel Eight. Thank you for your attention.

SCENE TWENTY-SEVEN

Brett is back on the clouds set with a George Burns look-a-like, and this time Missy is with him. Their conversation is all in thoughts, but their faces are seen on the screen when their words are heard, and their expressions mirror their thoughts.

BRETT

What happened to James Mason?

BURNS

He had to make an appearance with Eva Marie Saint and Cary Grant. The 62nd anniversary of *North by Northwest,* I think.

BRETT

Afterlife can be taxing, I guess.

BURNS

That was a fine presentation, Mr. Whitson. Our focus group scored you in the 80 percentile for content and 85 for presentation. The numbers might have been higher but there is still a good number of people who are afraid of the enormity of the change that is manifesting in the people of higher consciousness who got the vaccinations. Not everyone was ready to lead a low-conflict life or have their thoughts exposed. That said, they particularly liked Franklin. They thought he was a kick. They thought Missy did a lot to humanize Brett.

BRETT

That's a very discerning response, don't you think, sweetheart?

MISSY

(Smiling) I don't know that I humanize you, dear. I find you very human. But maybe you need that anchorman presence to get the information to the viewers. You're a young Uncle Walter.

BURNS

I think what it comes down to is that we all want a happy, safe, productive, creative world, and to get there we have much work to do.

BRETT

A utopian goal, but how do we get there from here?

MISSY

From what we've seen so far, darling, we don't have to know how. We simply have to appreciate what has already happened – evolving even beyond our imagination – and go with the flow. The answers will be there when they're needed. Brett, remember that favorite line of yours from Vonnegut. The young man who was asked about his future and he said that life is "one foot in front of the other -- through leaves, over bridges."

BRETT

Yes. And another image comes to mind. It's the scene toward the end of the Indiana Jones movie, the one with the Nazis. Indiana's last task to save his father – played by Sean Connery; he's been shot – is to cross an abyss which seems to have no bridge. But Indiana "knows" that there is a bridge and he takes a step forward and there it is, under his feet.

BURNS

Smart kids. You've seen what can happen in a matter of months and all of it for the good. The continuing shift is going to be even more precipitous than we might predict, but that's what is needed to get us to where we want to go. It has been essential to recruit the best and the brightest to manage the transformation, to pick up the proverbial reins. Because after the Earth is restored to its proper natural state, we will need all new leaders to update and maintain the new systems that conform with the environment and nurture the flora and fauna in a healthy way.

MISSY

(Shakes her head) It's fascinating how pie-in-the-sky this all sounds like, but it is so right that we should want it, and exciting that this is our path.

BURNS

Exactly, Ms. Blaine. And with that prescient observation, I infer that you share not only the goal but you inherently trust that your role in it will precisely match your skills. You both, along with others you will meet along the way, will indeed be excellent at explaining to others what is happening as the changes come about. Telling stories with vital metaphors embedded in them, touchstones for the trip ahead.

Burns is suddenly gone. Missy and Brett look at each other, shake their heads and smile.

MISSY

What did he mean when he said, "Goodnight, Gracie"?

BRETT

I haven't a clue. But he looked like he was pleased with our meeting and happy to be going home.

MISSY

So am I.

About the Author

Tony Seton is a journalist, writer, and publisher. An Emmy award-winning broadcast journalist for ABC Television News, he covered Watergate, six elections, and five space shots. And he produced Dan Cordtz's business/economics coverage and Barbara Walters' news interviews.

Later, Tony wrote and produced two award-winning public television documentaries.

Through Seton Publishing, Tony has written, designed, and published more than 45 of his own books and screenplays, and has edited and published 30-some books for clients.

As a political consultant, his clients have included Nancy Pelosi, Tom Campbell, John Vasconcellos, the American Nurses Association, and various local candidates.

He has taught journalism and writing, provided media training, and produced websites.

Tony is also a private pilot and a photographer.

SETON
PUBLISHING

www.ingramcontent.com/pod-product-compliance
Lightning Source LLC
LaVergne TN
LVHW050649100826
845148LV00011B/2051

* 9 7 8 1 7 3 7 5 9 3 2 0 1 *